The Chirping Band

By WonKyeong Lee
Illustrated by EunJoo Jang
Language Arts Consultant: Joy Cowley

NORWOOD HOUSE PRESS
Chicago, Illinois

DEAR CAREGIVER   MySELF Bookshelf is a series of books that support children's social emotional learning. SEL has been proven to promote not only the development of self-awareness, responsibility, and positive relationships, but also academic achievement.

Current research reveals that the part of the brain that manages emotion is directly connected to the part of the brain that is used in cognitive tasks, such as: problem solving, logic, reasoning, and critical thinking—all of which are at the heart of learning.

SEL is also directly linked to what are referred to as 21st Century Skills: collaboration, communication, creativity, and critical thinking. MySELF Bookshelf offers an early start that will help children build the competencies for success in school and life.

In these delightful books, young children practice early reading skills while learning how to manage their own feelings and how to be considerate of other perspectives. Each book focuses on aspects of SEL that help children develop social competence that will benefit them in their relationships with others as well as in their school success. The charming characters in the stories model positive traits such as: responsibility, goal setting, determination, patience, and celebrating differences. At the end of each story, you will find a letter that highlights the positive traits and an activity or discussion to help your child apply SEL to his or her own life.

Above all, the most important part of the reading experience is to have fun and enjoy it!

Sincerely,

Shannon Cannon

Shannon Cannon, Ph.D.
Literacy and SEL Consultant

Norwood House Press • P.O. Box 316598 • Chicago, Illinois 60631
For more information about Norwood House Press please visit our website at www.norwoodhousepress.com or call 866-565-2900.

Shannon Cannon – Literacy and SEL Consultant
Joy Cowley – English Language Arts Consultant
Mary Lindeen – Consulting Editor

Library of Congress Cataloging-in-Publication Data
    Lee, WonKyeong.
    The Chirping Band / by WonKyeong Lee ; illustrated by EunJoo Jang.
      pages cm. -- (MySelf bookshelf)
    Summary: "After being called lazy by the other bugs, the grasshoppers form The Chirping Band to prove them wrong. The band practices hard, singing and playing, preparing for their first concert. On the night of their concert, no one shows up. Determined, the band puts on their best performance and proves to the other bugs that they are hard-working"-- Provided by publisher.
    ISBN 978-1-59953-663-7 (library edition : alk. paper) -- ISBN 978-1-60357-723-6 (ebook)
    [1. Grasshoppers--Fiction. 2. Insects--Fiction. 3. Bands (Music)--Fiction. 4. Conduct of life--Fiction.] I. Jang, EunJoo, illustrator. II. Title.
    PZ7.1.L44Ch 2015
    [E]--dc23
                          2014030343

Manufactured in the United States of America in Stevens Point, Wisconsin.
263N—122014

Hi! I'm the conductor
of the famous Chirping Band.
It's a band of grasshoppers.
Listen and I will tell you
how it came to be.

4

5

I asked the other bugs
what they thought of grasshoppers.

"They're lazy!" said the honeybees.
"They sing all summer while we work!"

"Good for nothing!" said the ants.
"We work hard while they play!"

8

I was shocked by their words.

I called a meeting with the grasshoppers.

"We have a reputation for being lazy.

Let's show everyone that we can be useful."

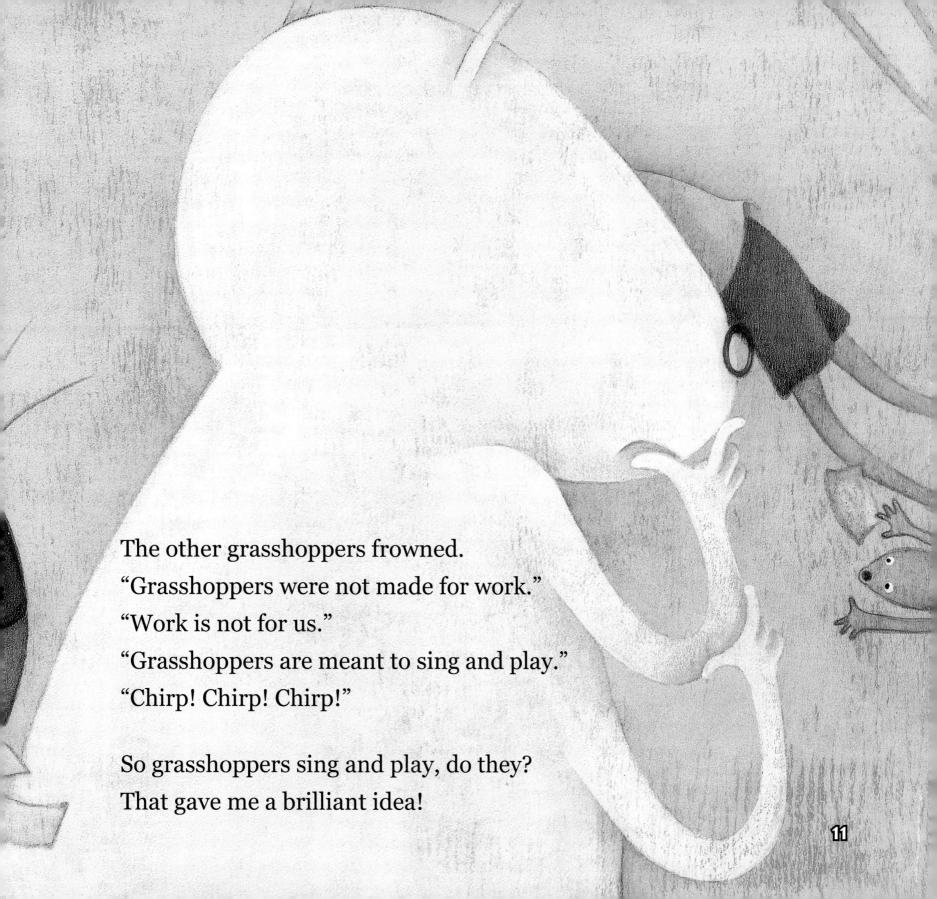

The other grasshoppers frowned.

"Grasshoppers were not made for work."

"Work is not for us."

"Grasshoppers are meant to sing and play."

"Chirp! Chirp! Chirp!"

So grasshoppers sing and play, do they?

That gave me a brilliant idea!

11

I said to the grasshoppers,
"If something was fun,
would you do it?"

"Do what?" they all said.

"Sing and play," I told them.

"That's easy," they said.
"It's what we do all day."

But grasshoppers are lazy.

They wanted to be in a band

but they didn't want to practice.

Some woke up late.

Some forgot to come.

Some forgot their instruments.

I refused to give up.

"Come to practice."

"Bring your instruments."

"Play, play, play."

"Do you call this a band?"

16

17

The grasshoppers got better.
As they improved,
they became more interested.
They even practiced by themselves.

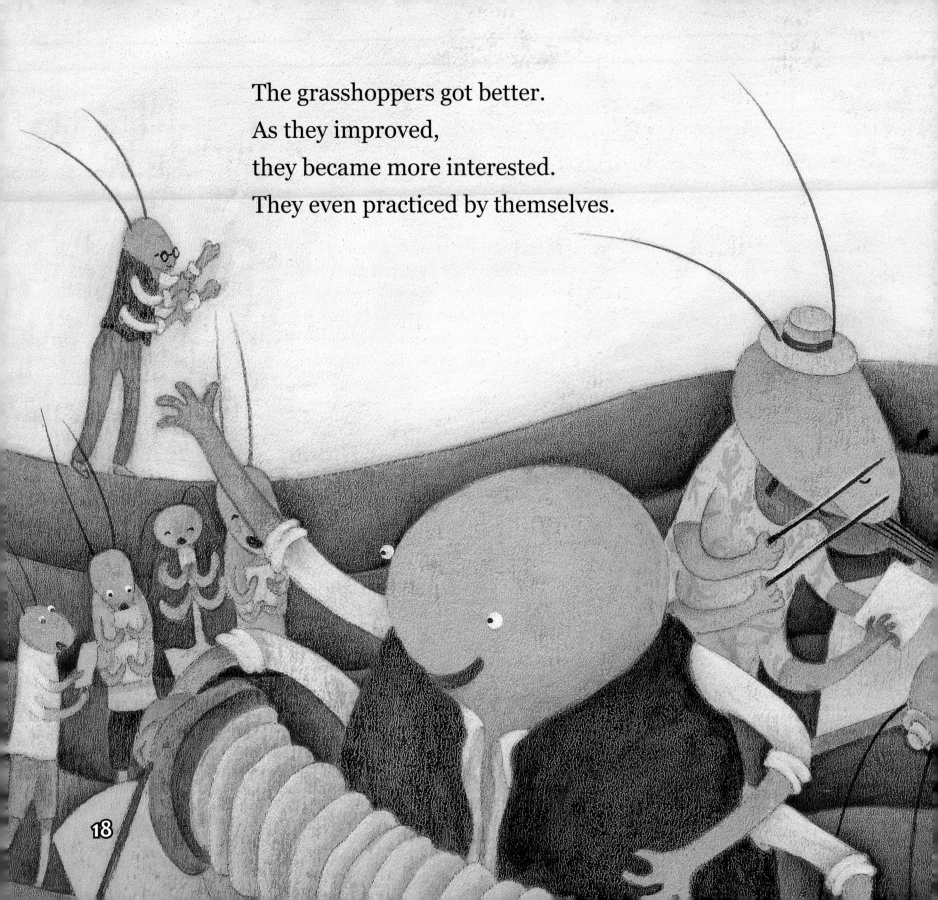

"Let's come early!" they said.
"Let's have more practice sessions!"

"Hurrah!" I said. "At last!
We have our Chirping Band!"

First Concert
of the
Chirping Band

Where: Open space in forest

When: Night of full moon

We put up a poster
for our first concert.
Then we started
to make a stage.

On the night of the concert,
we waited and waited.
But no one came.

It was only us.
But we had practiced hard
and so we decided to play anyway.

23

**Chirp! Chirp! Chirp! Chirp!
Twang! Twang! Twang!
Doo-doo! Doo-doo! Doo-doo!**

When we began to play,
all kinds of bugs came to hear.

24

It was a wonderful concert.

The bugs cheered and cheered.

"Wow! That was great!"

"You did a really good job!"

"That was the best concert we ever heard!"

After that, our Chirping Band
was the best band in the forest.
No one called us lazy grasshoppers.
We found out it was fun to work hard and
become good at something we enjoyed.

29

Dear Grasshoppers,

Tonight you gave a beautiful concert in the moonlight. I was so proud of how good you sounded and how our music made everyone happy.

I know that it took a lot of hard work and practice to make sure we sounded good when we played in our band. I know it's not always fun or easy to practice something that is difficult to do. But the only way to get better at something is to practice, even if it's not always fun. Sometimes you can find a way to make your work feel like fun, and sometimes you just have to make up your mind that you're going to work hard no matter what.

Your hard work made us a better band, and our band made lots of other bugs very happy. Making other bugs happy made us happy in turn. Good job, grasshoppers!

From your leader,
The Chirping Band Conductor

30

SOCIAL AND EMOTIONAL LEARNING FOCUS
Working Hard/Practicing

Have you ever heard the phrase, "Practice Makes Perfect"? That is true for the grasshoppers in the story and it can be true for you too! At first it might seem like a lot of work, but like the grasshoppers, you'll improve and become more interested. When you see how much better you are getting, you'll want to practice even more.

Think of something you would like to get really good at. For example, playing an instrument, reading, kicking a soccer ball, drawing, throwing a baseball, running fast, singing, or even learning your math facts.

Start with your baseline data. This means the starting point. On a separate piece of paper, you can record yourself singing or reading, measure how far you throw or kick a ball, keep track of the time it takes to run around the block or to complete a stack of math fact flashcards. Make a schedule to practice at least 20 times and keep track of your progress.

I'm On My Way to Running!

Date	How many	What I did
September 7	10 times	Number of times I ran around the school.
September 9	11 times	Tried to run an extra lap.
September 15	9 times	Need to keep practicing.
September 16	10 times	Made improvement running.
September 17	15 times	Achieved my goal for running.

Try this too … *(Continued on next page)*

Here are a few sayings you can use to make posters to keep you going:

- **Champions keep playing until they get it right.**

- **Tomorrow's victory is today's practice.**

- **Practice puts brains in your muscles.**

- **It's not necessarily the amount of time you spend at practice that counts; it's what you put into the practice.**

- **Don't practice until you get it right. Practice until you can't get it wrong.**

There might be days when you don't see a lot of improvement. Sometimes it takes several days before you notice the difference. There are also days when you might not be feeling your best, or maybe it was really hot outside and you didn't have the same amount of energy. Take notes to remember things about your practice sessions to help you in the future. At the end of 20 practice sessions, compare your baseline to your "finish" line!

Reader's Theater

Reader's Theater is an interactive approach to reading that allows students to understand each story through dramatic interpretation. By involving students in reading, listening, and speaking activities, they provide an integrated approach for students to develop fluency and comprehension. A Reader's Theater edition of this book is available online. You can access the script by scanning the QR code to the right or visit our website at: http://www.norwoodhousepress.com/chirpingband.aspx